Love Is Love

Written by Michael Genhart, PhD

Illustrated by Ken Min

I’ve got a problem.
Today some kids were laughing at my shirt.

They were teasing me for wearing it.
One of the kids said my shirt was gay.

My friend asked, “What does that mean?”
I wasn’t sure, but I think it’s because I have two dads.

I told my friend I don't like it when kids say that being gay is gross.
Or they say, "That's so gay!" when they don't like something.
Some of the kids even said my family wasn't a real family.
That's just mean. And it hurts.

My friend told me maybe I shouldn't wear the shirt.
But that doesn't seem fair.
I wonder why some people think I shouldn't have two dads. Why would they think being gay is wrong?

Maybe being different is scary to some people.
But my dads really love each other.

Just like my friend's mom and dad love each other.
That isn't different.

My dads got married on a mountaintop wearing skis!

My friend's mom and dad got married on a beach wearing bathing suits!

And my dads love me very much.
Just like my friend's mom and dad love her.
We both have families who love us.
That's not so different either.

I know lots of other gay people.
My teacher Mrs. Adams is gay.
Police Chief Carter is gay, too.
TWEET
And my sister's coach is gay.

Mayor Sanchez is also gay.

There are even lots of famous gay people. Singers and scientists and artists and athletes. My friend thinks we might have a gay president one day!

But some people believe being gay is something to be ashamed of. My dads told me that some gay people even try to pretend they aren't gay.

My dads say that no one should be ashamed of who they are. That's why this shirt is so special. My dads gave it to me. I feel good wearing it.

I love my dads and they love me. We're not so different from any other family. And I am not embarrassed about who we are.

So when some kids say, “Your dads are gay!”
I’ll just say, “Yes, they are!”

And when some kids say, “You’re not a real family!”
I’ll just say, “Yes, we are!”

My dads love me and I love my dads. That's what really matters. And I'm proud to be a part of my family.

Love is the same.

Wherever you live.

Whoever you are.

And whomever you love.

LOVE IS LOVE!

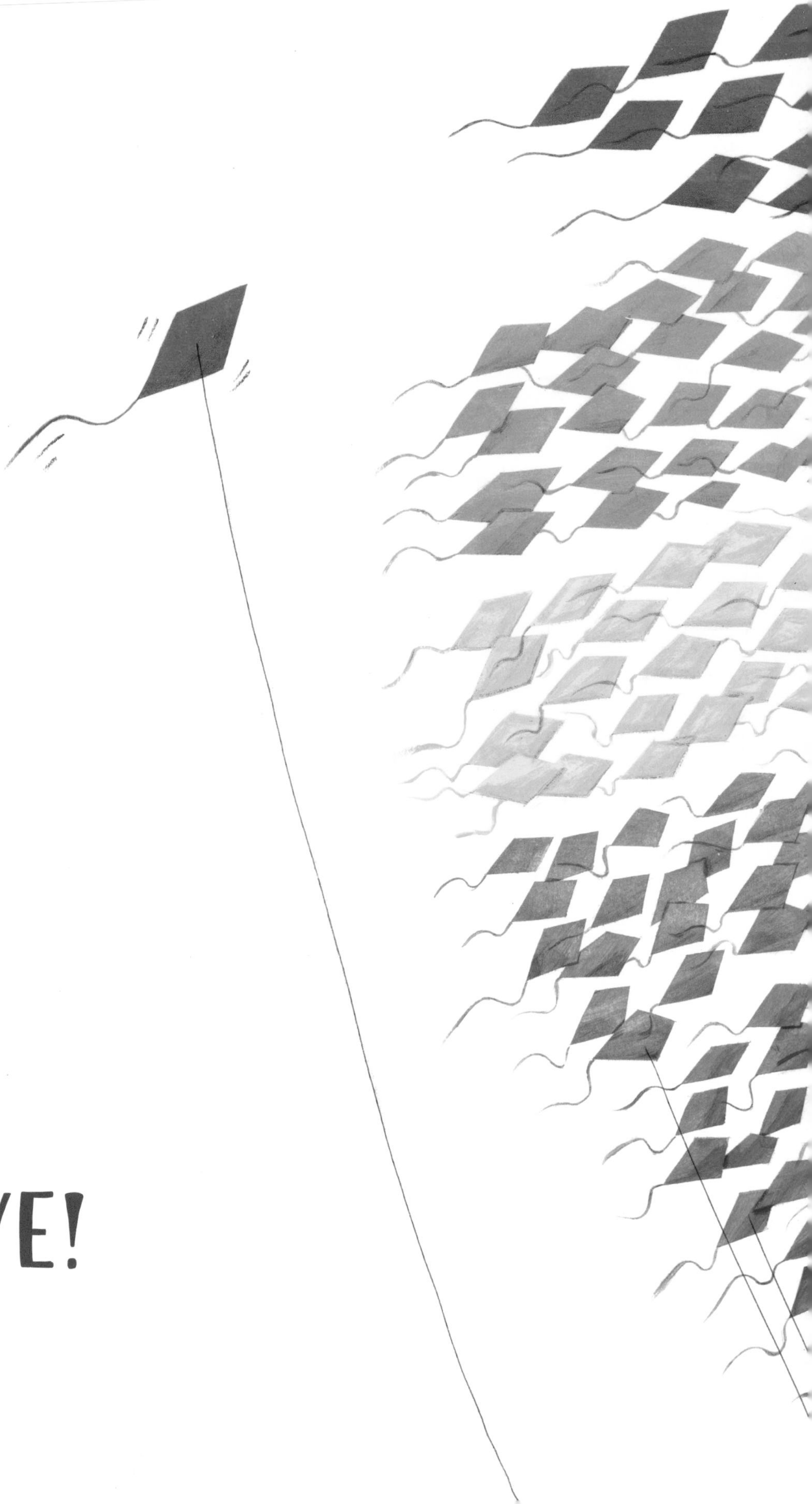

NOTE TO KIDS

In our story, our characters feature kids wearing a shirt with a rainbow heart on the front. The rainbow is often used as a symbol of pride for the LGBTQ (Lesbian, Gay, Bisexual, Transgender, Queer or Questioning) community. Gilbert Baker created this symbol of hope in 1978. He chose the rainbow because of its natural beauty and that you can see rainbows anywhere in the world and across all cultures. The colors of the rainbow are meant to represent all the different people in the gay community coming together—people of all ages, genders, races, and all the people who support them. The rainbow flag has become a powerful worldwide symbol of love and acceptance over the last forty years. Many people look to the flag to help them stand up, be visible, be proud, and be gay.

Not everyone finds it easy to be visible or to be proud of who they are. Like the characters in our book discussed, sometimes people act like being gay is a bad thing. Or that families with LGBTQ members aren't real families. Hopefully you have friends and family who support and love you. And we hope you're able to be proud of who you are, who your family members are, and who your friends are. But if you ever feel unsafe, it is important to find someone who can help. If you need help, you could go to a friend or a caring adult such as a parent, other family member, teacher, librarian, or counselor. There are also organizations that help kids deal with difficult situations and difficult emotions. Talk with a caring adult about which organization or resource might be right for you.

Above all, remember that being gay should never be a bad thing. Saying something is gay should not be used as an insult. As the characters in our story learn, being gay or having someone gay in your family or community is normal! And all loving families are real no matter what their family is made of. Love is love!

NOTE TO PARENTS, TEACHERS, AND OTHER CARING ADULTS

Throughout our history we've used hateful terms to depict various groups of people who are different from the majority, are without power, and are therefore easier to pick on. Hateful terms depicting those who identify as gay, lesbian, bisexual, transgender, queer, or any people whose gender presentation is non-traditional remain one of our society's current dilemmas. Marginalizing any group of people is wrong, as is the use of derogatory language toward anyone. Teaching this lesson to our children early in life can empower them to not remain silent and to correct these wrongs.

The spirit of this book is to help develop communities of children, across the globe, who will support each other emotionally and not create divisions (through hurtful speech or actions) of any kind. Children empowered to appreciate and respect similarities and differences between individuals are more likely to grow up to be teenagers who will hopefully do the same, and these teens will grow up to be young adults who maintain the same intolerance of cruelty or injustice toward anybody. It is easier to learn how to respect others when you are a child than to unlearn disrespect of others as an adult.

What does empowering children in this context mean? It means giving them guidance to deal with hurtful words that occur in conversations or exchanges between children. While we cannot make children be kind to one another, we can show them through action, intervention, and example how to be kind and empathic as well as how to contribute to a culture that is caring and respectful toward everyone. Ultimately, wouldn't it be nice to be part of a world where we can stop talking about being gay like it's a condition, something to fix, or something to apologize for?

Some people feel it's best to handle these kinds of (hurtful) exchanges by ignoring them, that you give away power by reacting to name-calling. I feel it's more important to help children act in respectful and responsible ways toward one another. In particular, we need intervention in the moment because kids are affected emotionally each time hurtful words are used. Sadly, with regard to anti-gay bullying, we are talking about a kind of social injustice, how targeted children can be excluded socially, resulting in heightened insecurity and lowered self-esteem, and sometimes far worse outcomes, including significant depression and suicidal ideas. Therefore, while *Love Is Love* gives children something to say that is affirmative, powerful, confident, and courageous, it is also important that kids know they have a safe place to go or a person who will always support them.

Helping children to stand up and give voice to doing the right thing is good for their character: creating integrity, courage, generosity, compassion, and empathy. You'll be helping to teach children how they can contribute to changing a significant social problem. Moreover, you'll be showing them that there's an equal place for everyone in this world.

ENCOURAGING CHILDREN TO TELL THEIR STORIES

As you read *Love Is Love* with a child, take the time to see how he or she is reacting. Feelings are often confusing and complex. The issues in this book may require not one, but many conversations. Please consider the following discussion ideas as ways of starting conversations, as well as appropriate strategies for intervening. Children are very creative, so they will likely be able to add much more to what you see here.

QUESTIONS TO INSPIRE DISCUSSION

- Have you ever felt excluded when you were in a group of children?
- Why were you excluded and how did that feel?
- Have you ever been the target of "hurtful words?" How did it make you feel? How did you respond and/or react?
- Did you feel like you could say something to the person who said those hurtful words?
- What are some reasons why a child might be mean to someone?
- What are some common words used to be mean to other kids?
- What does "gay" mean to you?
- What are some other "mean" words used to describe gay people (boys and girls)?
- Why are words like "that's so gay!" used to show dislike for someone or something?
- Do you know someone who is gay or lesbian?
- How do you think they would feel if someone made fun of them?
- Have you ever cared so much about someone who is gay that you would speak up for that person?
- What is a bystander? How does a bystander feel when he/she hears someone being teased?
- If you saw or heard someone being hurt with words, would you help out and be an ally? What would you say or do to help out and be an ally?
- What impact would it have to say/do something or to say/do nothing?
- If you ever felt like you were in danger because someone was using words or actions to make you feel unsafe, who are the caring adults you can talk to?

NOTE FROM THE AUTHOR

Writing *Love Is Love* is the nexus of several aspects of my life. As a clinical psychologist in California, I treat children, teens, and adults—particularly those who identify as LGBTQ and are dealing with issues unique to this identity; have questions about their sexual orientation or gender identity; are a same-sex couple and are looking to start a family or want to address ways of strengthening their relationship; or individuals grappling with any number of life's stressors where being gay is somewhat more in the background. I'm also an occasional guest speaker at local elementary, middle, and high schools where I talk about being gay and whatever that may mean to the particular student audience I'm visiting.

But most importantly, I am a husband and dad. I have wonderful memories of marrying my husband in 2008. We'd already been together twenty-two years. We held our ceremony at our home on a beautiful fall day with family and friends. But it was our almost thirteen-year-old daughter who stole the show as a guitarist and vocalist, singing some of our favorite songs. She had our guests in happy tears. My husband and I have been fortunate that our daughter, who's in college now, has always been a talker and (relatively speaking) a pretty open book, sharing all kinds of stories about her experiences.

What's common to these three areas of my world is that I've been privy to numerous stories that people have shared with me over time—all kinds of stories about all kinds of people. Gay and straight. Young and old. All races and religions. All kinds of families. In these stories I've noticed themes that emerge and re-emerge. It's these themes that inspired me to start writing children's books, *Love Is Love* in particular. Too many children I've met in my office or in schools don't know what to say in the face of anti-gay slurs. Too many gay adults carry around wounds, scars from a lifetime of hurts, even as they live relatively contented lives. And these pockets of hurt are interfering with people feeling safe, proud, important, and equal. I felt there needed to be a children's book showing that being gay is another kind of normal. Period. And I wanted to use the word "gay" as much as possible to help normalize it.

In thinking about *Love Is Love*, I've also reflected on my own stories—things I've heard or incidents I've witnessed that prove to me there's a need for a book like this. For example, I have heard kids in a swimming pool playing "smear the queer," a mom telling her son in a department store that the clothes he was picking out looked "too gay," a man at the gym shout across to a friend that the football player who'd fumbled a pass was "a total fag," and a high school student saying "that's so gay" about something he didn't like.

Of course, we all hear things of a similar nature. And so do our children. How is any of this okay? Shouldn't we all be offended? There's still some ugliness in the words we use at times. There's still too much permissiveness in the pejorative language some people use about gay people even in an era that's progressing toward greater equality. This is especially true on a global scale, where being gay remains completely unsafe and is seen as abnormal, pathological, or immoral, and is illegal in many places in the world. We will depend on the children of today and their leadership to be brave and step up, following their hearts and their moral compasses, to continue building a path of equality and non-discrimination. I wondered what a conversation between two kids might sound like today if one of them were being made fun of and turned to the other for help. So I wrote this story, which rests on the shoulders of all those whose stories I've heard, to offer a positive voice to children so they can help us all move our national and international conversations forward even further.

My goal is to help bring people together. I think the kids in *Love Is Love* do just that. This story is about a shared humanity based on love for the children's families. They discover and uncover their truth, our truth: love is love.

ADDITIONAL RESOURCES

Following are some organizations that can offer additional guidance and support for members of the LGBTQ community and their families and friends.

Born This Way Foundation – This organization is committed to supporting the wellness of young people and empowering them to create a kinder and braver world. Their aims include creating safe-spaces and more nurturing communities, offering opportunities to develop life skills, and providing improved mental health resources.

COLAGE: People with Lesbian, Gay, Bisexual, Transgender, and/or Queer Parents – Uniting people with lesbian, gay, bisexual, transgender, and/or queer parents into a network of peers and supporting them as they nurture and empower each other to be skilled, self-confident, and just leaders in our collective communities.

Family Equality Council – Focusing on changing attitudes and policies to ensure all families are respected, loved, and celebrated, especially those with parents who are lesbian, gay, bisexual, transgender or queer.

Gay, Lesbian & Straight Education Network (GLSEN) – Their mission is to ensure that every member of every school community is valued and respected regardless of sexual orientation, gender identity, or gender expression.

GroundSpark – Using their Respect For All Project, and films such as *That's A Family; It's Elementary; Let's Get Real;* and *Straightlaced*, GroundSpark aims to ignite change and develop inclusive, bias-free schools and communities.

Human Rights Campaign (HRC) – Their Welcoming Schools program is an LGBTQ-inclusive approach to addressing family diversity, gender stereotyping, and bullying in K-5 schools.

Parents, Families and Friends of Lesbians and Gays (PFLAG) – The nation's largest family and ally organization, started by a mother publicly supporting her gay son, now with over four hundred chapters across all fifty states plus Washington DC and Puerto Rico, is committed to advancing equality through support, education, and advocacy.

True Colors Fund – Their mission is to end homelessness among lesbian, gay, bisexual, and transgender youth and to create a world in which people can be their true selves.

ABOUT THE AUTHOR

Michael Genhart, PhD, has been a clinical psychologist in private practice in San Francisco and Marin for 25 years. During this time, he has specialized in working with children who have gay or lesbian parents, gay teens and coming out issues, same sex relationships, and LGBTQ parenting matters. Additionally, he has been a consultant to colleagues particularly with regard to working with the LGBTQ population. He has also spent the last fifteen years visiting and speaking at local elementary, middle, and high schools to engage students in conversations about LGBTQ issues. Michael Genhart is author of several other books for children including *I See You* and *Ouch! Moments*.

ABOUT THE ILLUSTRATOR

Ken grew up on the works of Margret and H.A. Rey, William Joyce, and DC Comics. He was born and raised in Los Angeles and studied illustration at ArtCenter College of Design. He has storyboarded for various commercials and animated TV shows such as *Wabbit! A Looney Tunes Production*, *Futurama*, and *The Fairly OddParents*. His illustration work has been recognized numerous times by the Society of Children's Book Writers & Illustrators (SCBWI). In 2012, the first picture book he illustrated, *Hot, Hot Roti for Dada-Ji*, received the Picture Book Honor Award for Literature from the Asian Pacific American Librarians Association (APALA). These days, you will find Ken illustrating, storyboarding, writing, and dreaming up stories for children.

To my real family, John and Gabby; to Rana, Emma, and Kelly who saw the potential in this story and helped make it even better; and to the many efforts, large and small, that are working toward creating a world where it is safe and normal to be gay. —MG

Text by Michael Genhart
Illustrations by Ken Min

Published by Little Pickle Press, an imprint of Sourcebooks Kids.
P.O. Box 4410, Naperville, Illinois 60567-4410
(630) 961-3900
sourcebooks.com
Library of Congress Cataloging-in-Publication Data is on file with the publisher.
Source of Production: Wing King Tong Paper Products Co. Ltd., Shenzhen, Guangdong Province, China
Date of Production: November 2021
Run Number: 5024198
Printed and bound in China.
WKT 10 9 8 7 6 5 4